Walt Disney's

The Donald Duck Book

HUEY LOUIE DEWEY

by **Daphne Davis**
illustrated by **Hawley Pratt** and **Al White**

A GOLDEN BOOK, New York
Western Publishing Company, Inc., Racine, Wisconsin 53404

Here is Donald Duck.

This is his house.
Look who is peeking out
the window.
It is Donald's
nephew Huey.

DONALD
DUCK

Here is Donald's backyard.
Look who is hiding
  up in the tree.
It is Donald's nephew Louie.

Here is Donald's garden.
Look who is hiding behind the wheelbarrow.
It is Donald's nephew Dewey.

"Hello, Uncle Donald."

Huey, Louie, and Dewey play leap frog in the yard.

They eat lunch.

After lunch they get ready
to go outside, but…it is raining!

So they hang up their jackets
and go upstairs to play.

Here is their playroom.

This is Huey's favorite toy.

This is Dewey's favorite stuffed animal.

This is Louie's favorite game.

Here comes Uncle Donald.
"Time for your nap, boys," he says.

Donald Duck tucks them in.
"Sweet dreams, Huey, Louie, and Dewey."